CHUPIE
The Binky That Returned Home

by **Thalia** • Illustrated by **Ana Martín Larrañaga**

based on characters created and designed by **Thalia**

A Celebra Children's Book • A member of Penguin Group (USA) Inc.

For my children, Sabrina Sakaë and Matthew Alejandro,
who inspired me to create *CHUPIE*.
And to the dozens of Binkies that I sent straight to Binkyland!
-Thalia

CELEBRA CHILDREN'S BOOKS
A division of Penguin Young Readers Group
Published by the Penguin Group
Penguin Group (USA) Inc., 375 Hudson Street, New York, New York 10014, USA

USA / Canada / UK / Ireland / Australia / New Zealand / India / South Africa / China
Penguin Books Ltd, Registered Offices: 80 Strand, London WC2R 0RL, England

For more information about the Penguin Group visit penguin.com

Library of Congress Cataloging-in-Publication Data

Thalia.
Chupie: the Binky that returned home / by Thalia ; illustrated by Ana Martín Larrañaga.
pages   cm
Summary: Sabrina loves her "binky" and takes it with her wherever she goes, until her mother tells a story
of a magical place called Binkyland, where a loving family and friends await each pacifier's return.
ISBN 978-0-451-41605-6 (hardcover)
1. Pacifiers (Infant care)—Fiction. 2. Babies—Fiction.] I. Martín Larrañaga, Ana, date- illustrator. II. Title.

PZ7.T314Chu 2013
[E]—dc23
2012050369

Printed in the United States

1 3 5 7 9 10 8 6 4 2

Designed by Jasmin Rubero
Text set in Banda Light with Chaloops

The publisher does not have any control over and does not assume
any responsibility for author or third-party websites or their content.

The illustrations were done with pencil and digital collage.

Sabrina loved her Binky. She took it everywhere.

She took it **shopping**

and to the **playground**,

and she always
slept with Binky.

One day, Mommy told **Sabrina**
that it was time to say good-bye to Binky.
Sabrina refused.

"Before you make up your mind,
would you like to hear a story?"
her mommy asked.
"It's about Binkyland."
"Binkyland?" asked Sabrina.
"Yes," Mommy answered.
"It is the magical home of the Binkies."

There once was a little Binky named **Chupie.**
He lived in **Binkyland,** where trees are lollipops
and clouds are cotton candy.

His home was a beautiful castle made out of **caramel**.

Chupie would do fun things all day.
He rode on the swings.

He played on the slide,

and he enjoyed his bubble bath.

And when it was time to go to bed,
Mommy and Daddy Binky sang lullabies.
Chupie loved his mommy and daddy Binky,
and they were a very happy family.

One day while they were on a family picnic,
Chupie saw a beautiful glowing butterfly,
and they started to play.

And before he knew it,
he was far away from home.
He had left Binkyland.

Binkyland

He did not know where he was,
but right in front of **Chupie** was a surprised baby.
"Hello!" said the smiling baby.
Chupie smiled back.

And from that moment on,
they became best friends.
They would spend all day together.

And if baby ever cried,

Chupie was there to calm him down.

One day, he asked **Chupie** if he had a family. **Chupie** thought of **Binkyland** and said, "Yes, I do. And I miss them very much."

Chupie needed his family . . . just like baby needed his.

So Mommy found a box for **Chupie** to ride back to **Binkyland**.

"Good-bye! I'll always remember you!"
And baby mailed **Chupie** home to **Binkyland**.

Meanwhile, everyone in **Binkyland** was sad. They all missed **Chupie**.

Suddenly, Chupie came back! Everyone in Binkyland was happy because Chupie was home . . .

and he never left again!

Sabrina thought for a moment.
"Can my Binky go to **Binkyland**, too?" she asked.
"Of course," said Mommy. "Of course."

That night, **Sabrina** went to bed with Binky in her heart and **Binkyland** in her dreams.

Dear Friends,

Would you like your child's Binky to go to **Binkyland**?

Then visit us on Facebook at Facebook.com/chupiethebinky. While you are there, post an image of your little one's pacifier and get advice on how others have succeeded in getting their child off the Binky. We would love to hear your story, too!

I look forward to seeing you there.

Love,

Thalia